D1386131

Adapted by Nancy E. Krulik
From the
Screenplay by Keith A. Walker and Corey Blechman
Story by Keith A. Walker

WARNER BROS. PRESENTS
IN ASSOCIATION WITH LE STUDIO CANAL+, REGENCY ENTERPRISES AND ALCOR FILMS A DONNER / SHULER-DONNER PRODUCTION A FILM BY SIMON WINCER
'FREE WILLY' JASON JAMES RICHTER LORI PETTY JAYNE ATKINSON AUGUST SCHELLENBERG AND MICHAEL MADSEN EDITED BY O. NICHOLAS BROWN
PRODUCTION DESIGNED BY CHARLES ROSEN DIRECTOR OF PHOTOGRAPHY ROBBIE GREENBERG, A.S.C. MUSIC BY BASIL POLEDOURIS CO - PRODUCERS PENELOPE FOSTER,
RICHARD SOLOMON AND JIM VAN WYCK EXECUTIVE PRODUCERS RICHARD DONNER AND ARNON MILCHAN STORY BY KEITH A. WALKER
SCREENPLAY BY KEITH A. WALKER AND COREY BLECHMAN PRODUCED BY JENNIE LEW TUGEND AND LAUREN SHULER-DONNER
DOLBY STEREO IN SELECTED THEATRES DIRECTED BY SIMON WINCER

FANTAIL BOOKS

Published by the Penguin Group
Penguin Books Ltd, 27 Wrights Lane, London W8 5TZ, England
Penguin Books USA Inc., 375 Hudson Street, New York, New York 10014, USA
Penguin Books Australia Ltd, Ringwood, Victoria, Australia
Penguin Books Canada Ltd, 10 Alcorn Avenue, Toronto, Ontario, Canada M4V 3B2
Penguin Books (NZ) Ltd, 182–190 Wairau Road, Auckland 10, New Zealand

Penguin Books Ltd, Registered Offices: Harmondsworth, Middlesex, England

First published in the United States by Scholastic Inc. 1993
First published in Great Britain by Fantail 1994
3 5 7 9 10 8 6 4

Fantail Film and TV Tie-in edition first published 1994

FANTAIL

It was going to be a beautiful day. The orange and pink rays of the sun were already warming the waters of the Pacific Ocean. The whales were playing – diving down deep into the water. Then, as if out of nowhere, the black and white bodies would shoot out of the ocean, fountains of water exploding from their blow-holes.

One whale was off by himself. He was the one known as Three Spots. If he had known about the whaling boats, Three Spots might have stayed closer to his family on this particular morning.

Before he knew it, Three Spots was caught in a tight, heavy whaling net. "WHAW!" Three Spots cried out in fear. He twisted to the left and to the right. But it was no use. No matter which way he turned, the proud orca could not free himself. The speed boats captured the mighty whale and took him to the Northwest Amusement Park. Three Spots was far from his family and everything he had ever known. His captors had even changed his name to Willy.

Willy wasn't happy at the amusement park. The owner and his partner were mean men. And even though there were some people at the park who seemed to care about the orca, Willy wasn't ready to trust any humans, yet.

Then, one day, a new worker came to the park. He was a boy, around twelve years old. His name was Jesse. And like Willy, he no longer had a family.

Jesse was staying with Glen and Annie Greenwood, the young owners of a motor repair shop. But they weren't his real parents. Over the years, Jesse had lived in many foster homes with many different families. But none of them had become *his* family. Glen and Annie seemed nicer than the rest, but Jesse still didn't trust them. In fact, like Willy, Jesse didn't trust anybody.

Jesse's job at the amusement park was to scrub the graffiti from the walls outside Willy's tank.

One day, while Jesse was cleaning, he heard a loud whooshing sound coming from the whale's tank. Jesse whirled around in time to see Willy bash up against the side of the tank. Then, just as quickly as he had come, the giant whale disappeared into the dark blue water of the tank.

Where did the whale go? Jesse had to find out. Quietly, the boy made his way to the trainer's platform above the tank and peered over the edge. But the whale was nowhere to be seen!

Suddenly Jesse heard a groan! The mighty whale leapt out of the tank. Jesse stared in awe as the whale opened his mouth and fiercely showed off his sharp white teeth. The whale was amazing! Jesse had never seen anything like him in his whole life.

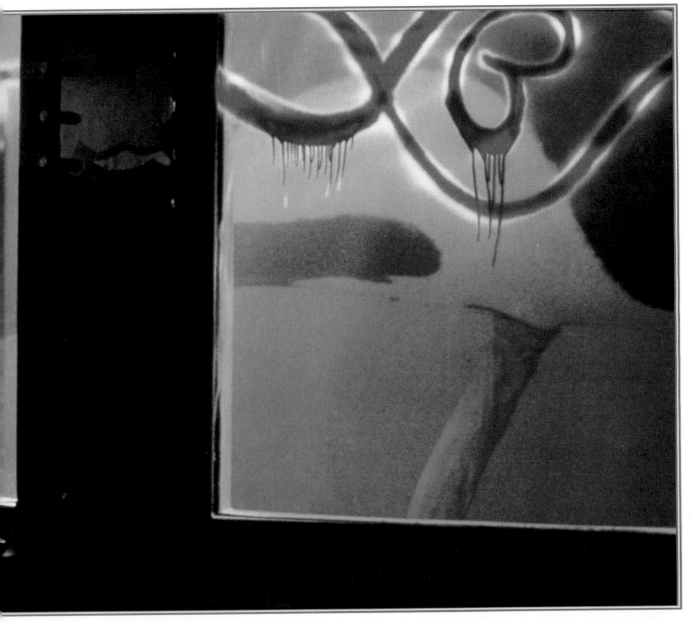

"What are you doing up there?" Randolph, the park caretaker, asked as he climbed on to the platform behind Jesse. "He's over seven thousand pounds that one," Randolph said, pointing towards the whale. "Got enough power in those jaws to crush your bones to dust!"

Jesse knew he would have to be careful. But that didn't mean he couldn't just sit and watch Willy swim. There was something about the whale that made Jesse think they could be friends. But he wasn't sure. After all, Jesse didn't have many friends.

All too soon, Jesse finished his job cleaning the walls of the park. Jesse wasn't going to miss the job that much, but he was going to miss Willy. Jesse wanted one last chance to talk to Willy the only way he knew how. So that night, while Glen and Annie were asleep, Jesse sneaked out of the Greenwoods' house and ran to the observation deck above Willy's tank.

Carefully, Jesse took a seat on the rim of the tank. He pulled out his harmonica and played a few notes. Willy got his message. The majestic whale leapt up to greet the boy. Jesse was thrilled! He was about to play a few more notes when he heard Randolph coming into the empty amphitheatre.

Randolph flipped on the lights. As Jesse tried to leap out of the way, he slipped and fell head first into the whale tank – dangerously near the 7000-pound killer whale!

Jesse's head hit the side of the tank. He fainted. Slowly his body began to sink into the darkness of the water. Suddenly an enormous creature appeared behind him. It was Willy! A killer whale!

With a single movement, the whale caught Jesse on his back and rolled the boy on to the platform again!

Willy had saved Jesse's life!

Randolph heard a thud as Jesse tumbled on to the platform. The caretaker ran to the theatre area and flicked on the lights again. Randolph rushed to Jesse's side, picked him up, and carried the boy to his tiny cottage in the corner of the park.

"Willy doesn't like visitors in his tank," Randolph said, after he had given Jesse a warm blanket and a cup of hot coffee.

"What were you doing in there?"

Jesse frowned. "Saying goodbye," he answered sadly. "I don't want to say goodbye to him."

Randolph smiled. He had an idea. Maybe Jesse wouldn't have to say goodbye to his new friend after all.

Randolph drove Jesse to the Greenwoods' house. "Looks like your parents are still up," he said.

"They're not my parents," Jesse answered gruffly.

Maybe not, but inside the house Glen and Annie were *very* worried about Jesse. They thought he'd run away!

"Jesse, what happened?" Annie asked.

Jesse looked at the floor. "I was at work," he mumbled.

"Hey, folks," Randolph interrupted. "I've been supervising Jesse down at the park. He's been doing a really good job." He winked at Jesse. "The thing is, we could use him for the rest of the summer, if that's all right with you."

The very next morning Jesse was back at the Northwest Amusement Park. It was time to feed Willy. Jesse was so glad to be near the whale, he didn't even mind handling the smelly dead fish that would be Willy's lunch! Jesse threw one of the dead fish into the water. On cue, the giant whale swam for the fish and caught it in his mouth.

But Willy didn't eat the fish. He tried to give it back to Jesse! "You want me to put the fish in your mouth?" Jesse asked the whale. Willy swam right up to Jesse and opened his huge mouth. Jesse stared at the rows of sharp teeth. With a smile, Jesse grabbed a handful of fish and put them into Willy's mouth.

Willy gobbled up the fish.

"I'll see you later, Will," Jesse said. "I have work to do." But as the boy stepped backwards, an amazing thing happened. The whale copied him and swam backwards too.

Jesse laughed. He stepped to the left.

Willy moved to the right.

Jesse did a headstand.

Willy stood on his head – his giant tail flipping and flopping out of the water.

Jesse danced.

Willy twirled in the water.

Jesse stuck out his tongue.

So did Willy.

Rae, the park's animal trainer, and Randolph were watching in the distance.

"I think Willy has finally found himself a soul mate here," Randolph said.

Rae smiled. Wade and Dial, the owners of the park, had been complaining that Willy cost them too much money. If Jesse could get Willy to put on a show, Wade and Dial would make enough money from the shows to build a larger tank for Willy.

Rae walked over to Jesse to talk to him about her idea. "Dial won't build Willy a bigger tank unless he thinks it will make him more money," she said simply. "What do you think about helping with that?"

Rae didn't have to ask twice. There was nothing Jesse wouldn't do to help Willy. The very next day, Rae and Jesse were on the trainer's platform trying to get Willy ready for his big show.

"Most orcas love to play around and do tricks," Rae explained. She handed Jesse a brightly coloured circle. "This is a target. Willy is supposed to respond to it and learn to follow it. When we work on a trick you have to reward him with some fish."

Jesse held up the target. Willy glanced over at it, then turned away. Jesse sighed. This was going to take longer than he'd thought. But Jesse wouldn't give up.

Finally, Rae decided Willy was ready to put on a show. But this first show would be for a very small audience – just two men – Wade and Dial. Willy had to prove that he could put on a terrific performance – and make money for the park!

Jesse took his place on the trainer's platform. "Would you like to do some tricks?" Jesse asked the whale. Then he reached down and placed a ball in Willy's mouth. Willy blew it back to Jesse. Then Jesse gave Willy a signal. Right on cue, the whale rolled over on his back.

It was time for Willy's big finish. Jesse took a deep breath. He moved his hand down and then up again. Willy knew what that meant. Immediately the giant orca swam around the pool, until finally he leapt up on to the platform next to Jesse!

Jesse smiled proudly. He knew Willy had done well. Now, if only Wade and Dial would agree.

It seemed to Jesse that Dial was taking an awfully long time to make up his mind. But finally he snapped his fingers and said simply, "Set it up. OK."

On the morning of Willy's first big show, Jesse took his place on the trainer's platform. The musical fanfare sounded from the arena. *Doo Too Doo Too!* It was time for the show!

As the crowd cheered, Jesse looked out into the audience. He couldn't see them, but he knew Glen and Annie Greenwood were there – just like *real* parents would be. Randolph and Rae were there, too. Jesse smiled. He and Willy were going to make them proud!

Jesse gave Willy the first signal. Immediately the whale sank gracefully down into the water. Jesse closed his hand into a fist and gave Willy the signal to rise up again. Only this time, the whale ignored him.

"Willy. You know the signals," Jesse said. "Come on."

Willy looked up at Jesse with sad eyes. But he wouldn't move. The noise upset him. Kids were shouting and banging loudly on the glass surrounding his tank.

"Boo!" Someone in the back row began to jeer. Soon the whole crowd was booing Willy. The show was a disaster.

After the show, Jesse didn't want to talk to anyone. He thought the whole mess was his fault! There was only one thing to do – run away! So Jesse packed up everything he owned, and waited until Glen and Annie were asleep. Then he climbed out of his bedroom window and headed for the park.

25

When Jesse got there, he found Willy looking sadly out towards the ocean. There, in the distance, Jesse saw a magnificent sight. A pod of killer whales was gathered, singing their whale song. It was Willy's family. They were calling to the whale they knew as Three Spots!

Jesse's attention was drawn away from the whales by lights flickering under the water. What could it be? Jesse ran downstairs to the observation window to take a look. He couldn't believe his eyes. Wade and a friend were drilling a hole in Willy's tank!

Quickly, Jesse ran to Randolph's house. "Wake up!" he cried as he knocked on the door. "There's a hole in Willy's tank. *They're trying to kill Willy!*"

That's when Jesse got the idea. "Hey, Randolph," he said. "Let's free Willy!"

Randolph didn't need convincing. But he did need help. So he called Rae.

It wasn't going to be easy to move a scared, 7000-pound killer whale. First they had to get the whale on to a trailer. Then they would need a tow truck to pull the trailer.

Jesse knew where they could get a tow truck! He and Randolph went to the Greenwoods' house. Jesse ran into the kitchen and grabbed the keys to Glen's truck from inside the cabinet. In less than a minute Randolph and Jesse were in the tow truck, thundering down the road towards the park.

Once the trailer was hitched to the tow truck, Randolph started the engines and headed towards Dawson's Marina. There they would set Willy free.

Everything was going fine until the police called Dial to tell him that Willy had been stolen! "This is a disaster!" Dial shouted. "We don't have theft insurance on the whale!"

Meanwhile, Glen was sure his tow truck had been stolen. He and Annie were driving in their car searching for it when Jesse's voice came over the car's CB radio.

"What are you doing with my truck?" Glen asked once he met up with Jesse, Randolph and Rae.

Jesse explained the situation. "Help us get him in the water, please," he begged.

Glen looked from Jesse to the whale. He couldn't say no.

Willy was very sick. He had been out of the water far too long.

Glen put his foot on the accelerator and the tow truck picked up speed. He gave a sigh of relief as the marina came into view. His joy didn't last long. Dial and his men were standing outside the marina gates; they were determined to keep Willy and his friends from getting into the water.

Glen pushed the accelerator pedal to the floor, and slammed the tow truck past Dial and his men, and through the gates – right into the water!

Willy was in the ocean now, but Dial's men had set up nets all along the shallow water of the marina. The only way Willy could get past them to deeper water was to leap over a high stone breakwater wall.

Jesse knew it was now or never for the whale. He scrambled on to the stone wall and gave Willy the signal to jump. Immediately, the whale dived deep into the water and began to speed out towards the wall.

Rae looked nervously at the tall breakwater wall. "Have you ever seen Willy jump that high?" she asked Randolph.

"Things can happen," he answered her.

"I love you, Willy," Jesse called out, one last time.

The beautiful killer whale was a blur now – swimming faster than a torpedo. And then he exploded into the air! He arched his magnificent black and white body over the stone wall. With a great splash, Willy landed in the free and open ocean.

Jesse watched his first friend swim out to join his family. But Jesse did not feel alone. For as Glen and Annie walked towards the stone wall to join him, Jesse thought that maybe, just maybe, he had finally found a family, too.